TO BEGIN AT THE BEGINNING

1:17 PM ON TUESDAY, APRIL 22, IN THE YEAR 2025

THE UNIVERSE BEGAN

Cosmologist Dr. Robert Porter is having a crisis of faith. Not of a faith he has lost, but of a faith he has gained. Robert now knew for a fact that the universe did not come into existence 13.8 billion years ago but rather precisely at what every person in the greater Los Angeles area would have considered to be 1:17 PM on Tuesday April 22 in the year 2025 but was actually second one of hour one of day one of week one of month one of year one of the existence of the universe. Robert did not doubt that fact. In fact, he had total faith that it was true.

PRAISE FOR STEVEN PAUL LEIVA

"Steven Leiva not only promises but delivers. Bravo!" — **Ray Bradbury**

"The author's true strength is in storytelling." — **Ricky L. Brown,** *Amazing Stories Magazine*

"Leiva has such a vivid imagination." — **Stuart Nulman,** *Montreal Times*

"Leiva is witty and engaging, stylistically striking." — **Areyon Jolivette,** *The Daily Californian*

"Steven Paul Leiva is a master wordsmith able to take on any genre or blend them." — **Jean Rabe,** *USA Today* **Bestselling Author.**

"Leiva (has a) genuine and impressive flair for originality and the kind of narrative-driven storytelling that fully engages the reader from beginning to end." — **Midwest Book Review.**

"Leiva's immense gifts for mystery and suspense are matched only by his wry biting wit." — **Paul Provenza, author of** *¡Satiristas!*

TO BEGIN AT THE BEGINNING

A Novella

With a Beginning, a Middle, and an End

TO BEGIN AT THE BEGINNING

A Novella

With a Beginning, a Middle, and an End

Steven Paul Leiva

Magpie

Press

Los Angeles, California

ISBN: 979-8-218-90969-7. 979-8-218-90969-7

Library of Congress Control Number: 2026900330

Cover Design by: Juan Padrón
https://www.juanjpadron.com/

Published in Los Angeles, California
Printed in the United States of America

DEDICATION

For Dave Doody

A Travel Agent to the Stars

ACKNOWLEDGMENTS

THE AUTHOR WISHES TO THANK

DONALD J. BINGLE FOR ALWAYS BEING THERE.

JEAN RABE FOR HER UNSTINTING SUPPORT
AND WRITERLY WISDOM.

HIS WIFE, AMANDA MARTIN, FOR HER LOVE
AND INCREDIBLY GOOD HUGS.

OUR CAT, MR. RAZZLEBERRY UNDERFOOT, JUST
BECAUSE.

AND MY TWENTY-SOMETHING
SELF WHOSE UNPUBLISHED SHORT STORY WAS
THE INSPIRATION FOR THIS NOVELLA.

1

As he remembered it...

He had woken up ridiculously early the day before because he was the guest speaker at that week's SoCal Breakfast Club meeting, which meant he had to be at their clubhouse by seven to partake in the community breakfast before he would speak to the members full of coffee, pancakes, eggs, oatmeal, sausages, and bacon on the "Evolution of the Universe: From the Big Bang to Today." It was a presentation he had given many times, but usually at a more reasonable, not to mention humane, hour of the day. But for him to expect a breakfast club to meet at any other time than early morning was, of course, unreasonable. However, that did not stop him from devoutly wishing it had been the SoCal Brunch Club. And that it had not been located in Santa Monica, miles away from his home in Pasadena.

Still, he had to admit that it was a pleasant sensation to walk into the welcoming griddle-warmth and appetizing smells of the clubhouse at 6:45 AM and find a large sign at the entrance to the dining hall that read:

TODAY'S SPEAKER

COSMOLOGIST DR. ROBERT PORTER

They had asked for a photo and Caltech's Office of Strategic Communications sent the one they had on file of Robert standing on the grounds of the Keck Telescopes in Maunakea, Hawaii. He was a tad younger then, and he hoped his face didn't show that he was now a tad older, which proved to him that vanity was not an unknown quantity in the hoped-for objective sciences.

He was greeted by the president of the club, Millie Formosa, who escorted him to his seat at the head table. Everyone already seated at the table welcomed him with thanks for coming and one of them then led him to the buffet table where he loaded up on scrambled eggs, sausages, some sliced fruit, and rye toast with plenty of butter and marmalade on the side. The conversation at the table was pleasant, if slightly awkward as all such conversations with the latest stranger tended to be.

Then it was the time for Robert to speak. Millie Formosa rose and went to the speaker's stand, welcomed everyone, thanked the wonderful cooking staff, made some necessary announcements, then introduced Robert with remarks based on his official Caltech bio.

Robert stood to the sound of warm applause (everything here was warm), moved to the speakers stand, thanked Millie for her introduction, and began.

"Well, hello, it's good to be here, and I thank you for the invitation. As your president Millie mentioned, I am a cosmologist, which is not to be confused with a cosmetologist. As a cosmologist I am concerned with the make-up of the universe. Whereas a cosmetologist is concerned with the make-up of the lovely faces of wonderful ladies. I sometimes think I went in the wrong direction as the universe is essentially cold and uninviting, whereas wonderful ladies are always warm and inviting."

Appreciative chuckles and even some full laughs were Robert's reward.

He then began his lecture by asking for the first of a series of digital slides he had emailed Millie the week before, and said, "Most of you have probably heard of *The Big Bang Theory*."

This opening statement was greeted by appreciative laughter. Robert mocked confusion over this, then turned to the first slide being displayed on the large video monitor behind him. On it was a picture of the cast of the late, lamented TV series. Robert chuckled his well-rehearsed chuckle and turned back to the audience. "No, I do not mean the CBS TV sitcom of the same name, as much as I adored it. I mean our current understanding of the origin and history of the universe, which some scientists prefer to call 'the Big Bang Model.' Robert turned back to the screen and Leonard, Sheldon, Penny, Howard and Raj were replaced by an illustrated diagram of the 13.8 billion years history of the evolution of the universe, starting with the big bang and ending at this very moment. "That's better. Not as funny, but more illustrative of what I will be talking about."

Robert then took the audience on a journey of

the nearly incomprehensible facts of the matter, which, of course, are the facts of matter, including the miniscule matter of our own flesh and blood matter. He covered the big bang itself, 13.8 billion years ago, which was less an actual bang (big or small) than a sudden something out of nothing existence. This lead, he explained to a moment of time, less than a second in fact, in which only a seething hot, dense fluid of particles constantly moving and colliding with each other and emitting all kinds of radiation was all that the universe contained. This, he explained was the building blocks of all structures we can now see in the universe. Because those colliding particles began moving away from each other as space was expanding—and cooling. But some smaller particles did stick to other smaller particles and formed bigger particles which combined with others to form nuclei. Those nuclei combined with electrons to create atoms and then the universal race began, so to speak, with matter aborning into stars and galaxies and everything we see today, including all life slithering, swimming, crawling, hopping, walking, and running on our very own earth. All of this the projected chart behind him illustrated by separating this evolution into eras—the Era of Particles; the Era of Nuclei; The Era of Atoms; the Era of Stars and Galaxies—each era lasting longer and longer from seconds to minutes to millions of years to billions of years.

Next Robert briefly mentioned the mind-bending concepts of the physics of quantum mechanics, relativity theory, and string theory, and how they all related to the history of matter, which was the history of the universe.

Robert's audience was made up of mainly middle-aged men and women, most of them in their late, retiring middle-age, rather than still active, height-of-their-powers middle-age. The kind of people with the time to give into curiosity. All were politely attentive, some were wide-eyed with wonder, others glared at Robert and his slides with skeptically squinted eyes.

But all gave Robert appreciative applause as he wrapped up quoting J. B. S. Haldane, "The universe is not only queerer than we suppose, but queerer than we can suppose."

Then Millie thanked Robert for a fascinating talk and opened up the floor for questions.

Robert hated this bit the most. For you cannot hit unaware people with this much nearly incomprehensible awareness without forcing up obvious questions.

One woman in a pink pants suit and a brilliant purple scarf asked: "How do scientists know all this?"

"Well," Robert gave the answer he always

gave, the only one he could give, "that would take a whole other talk to fully answer. In fact, it would take a comprehensive course in the scientific method to answer, but suffice it to say, it takes observation, research, theorizing, testing, experimenting, all the tools that human intellect can come up with formed into a methodical, repeatable, and testable method of inquiry. Which I know is not really a satisfying answer, it almost sounds like a great mystic's mumble-jumble to justify his or her pronouncements. But none-the-less, that's the truth."

A man stood up, a late-middle aged man in a checkered shirt and new, deeply blue, blue jeans, totally bald but with a full, compensating thick graying beard, and asked, "Where is God in this so-called history of yours."

Robert smiled a slight smile that was on the verge of being patronizing, for this was a question that had never once been in the left field.

"Well, it is not *my* history, it is just simply the history of the universe as we can best understand at the current time. Now, as to the question of God, I assume you mean the Judeo-Christian God?"

"Well, of course. I mean specifically the *Christian* God."

"Okay, great, thanks, I just wanted to clarify that because in human history more than 20,000 gods have been worshiped, most now forgotten, of course."

"False gods, every one of them!" The checkered-shirted man stated.

"Oh, is that the reason? Oh, okay. Well, that does simplify things. Let me try to answer your question this way: Science deals only with provable data. All our assumptions, theories, and conclusions rest on data, it always comes down to data. And the history of our universe has been written in data, data that we can observe and test and base experiments on. And in all the time we have been searching for and discovering data about the reality and history of the universe we have never discovered nor observed even one bit of data, or as some of my colleagues would superfluously say, not one data point that points to your Christian God, or any supernatural entity for that matter, having any participation in this history. Now, that does not mean that there has not been or even continues to be a god of any sort responsible for the universe, it just means we have never observed or discovered any data that would lead us to that conclusion."

"Are you telling me that a glorious sunrise is not data that proves God?"

That was a question Robert had never heard before. "Well, I would think a glorious sunrise is more likely to be data proving that the Earth rotates on its axis and is an indication of certain atmospheric conditions at that moment."

"But—"

"George!" Millie stopped George. "Let someone else ask a question."

"Yes!" someone in the back of the room yelled out and many in the audience applauded. George was obviously a well-known quality at the SoCal Breakfast Club.

Another man in gray slacks and a sweatshirt with a picture of Marvin the Martian on it, stood up as asked, "Do you believe in aliens?"

"Yes, I do!" Robert said unequivocally. "In fact an extremely nice and efficient one has been cleaning my house for ten years. But don't call ICE on me, Maria is legal, she has her visa."

"No, I mean, space aliens."

"Oh, okay, I get it. "Do I believe that there is life on other planets? No. Because I don't "believe" in anything I cannot see or discover through the scientific method. Now that doesn't mean there is not life on other planets, it simply means, I, *and no one else*, have ever seen data indicating such. But if there is life out there, I highly suspect that they have never visited us in flying saucers or even spinning teacups, because I highly doubt Earth is interesting and inviting enough even for an accidental traveler."

"But if you had to guess?" the questioner insisted.

"Guessing is for gamblers."

"Sylvia." Millie called out to a small woman in a floral print dress who had patiently had her hand up during all this.

Syvia stood up, excited to be recognized. "Mr.— I mean Dr. Porter; don't you think that religion and science are equally valuable as worldviews."

"No, Syvia, I do not. For religion has two aspects I find disturbing. One, it depends on faith, not facts. And two, it is a worldview that is not open to alteration in the face of facts."

"But you have faith in science, so what's the difference?"

"No, that is incorrect. One does not have faith in science. One has trust in the scientific method that, if correctly applied, it will point to data and facts that allow for a view of the reality, the 'what is' of the universe and all the wonders it contains, from the largest galaxies to the smallest molecules, and, at least here on Earth, in the variety and in most cases delight of life."

There were a few more questions, then Millie called the breakfast club meeting closed. Robert, after thanking Millie, tried to make a hasty exit, but several in the audience hung around to approach him and ask more questions. He answered them as best as he could, suggested some good popular science books on his subject to several people, thanked everybody again, then made his escape.

It was going to be a long drive home north on the 405 then east onto the 101, connecting to the 134, connecting to the 210, numbers, all numbers denoting pathways containing too many numbers of moving vehicles—cars and trucks and buses and the occasional annoying motorcycle—trying to get to work and school and shops and delivery destinations on time, a mass, a group, a hoard of humans in rolling metal, each so alike yet all so different, and each convinced that this, this existence, this reality, this "what is" was their own individual story.

Robert couldn't wait to get home to Pasadena, and yet he knew he and his wife, Elisabeth—Liz to him—would soon be back on the road for an even longer flow along the wide asphalt ribbon.

For his uncle Herold had died and his funeral was today in a little white clapboard church (Robert assumed) some 150 miles from Pasadena.

The call came in four evenings before from Maggie, Herold's wife. "Robert, your Uncle Harry died this morning." Maggie was the only one who called Herold Harry. Herold preferred to be Herold. Robert was saddened, Herold had been his favorite uncle, is mother's younger brother, a person absolutely no one ever disliked (the same could not be said of Maggie), he was tall, genial, had two generous helping hands for all, liked his sports, liked his beer, like his small cabin cruiser when he had had one when he and Maggie and the kids lived on the shore in Santa Barbara instead of many miles inland in Lompoc. Maggie gave him the when and where of the funeral and Robert noted them on the pad of paper that he always kept on the side table by his recliner in his den.

After he shed some tears and Liz comforted him with a hug, he asked her, "Do we have to go?"

"Bob, he was your favorite uncle."

"I know but—"

"Maggie," Liz accurately guessed.

Maggie was what use to be called a real go-getter, a person involved in everything within her orbit, a member of so many clubs she kept a notebook on each one on them, a church choir director after receiving a master's in music after her kids were self-sufficient, a local Republican Party organizer, the head of her Neighborhood Watch, and a decent cook. She always looked her best, her hair was always coiffured, she knew how to dress a woman of her build, which was always large and sometimes fat. And she was a natural born proselytizer for more than just her religion (she had once sold Avon products door-to-door to help pay for her college education), but her religion was at the top of her list. Maggie's basic philosophy of life was that what was good for her should be good for everyone.

Robert's early (at the age of sixteen) declaration that he was an atheist came as a shock to Maggie. And yet she found it understandable. Harry's sister, Robert's mother, was never much of a religious woman. She didn't deny the existence of God, but having spent her teen years with a grandmother living in the house who was a bible-thumper of the most trumpery sort, she was not fond of people sermonizing her. "You can Simonize my car, but don't sermonize my soul," she was fond of saying, considering herself a bit of a wit. But the fact that his mother was lost was no reason why her son should be. So one day when Robert was nineteen, Maggie drove from Santa Barbara to the East San Gabriel Valley where Robert's family lived to take him out to lunch at the local Denny's to try to save his soul. She didn't succeed. But Robert did enjoy his Denny's Deluxe Sandwich.

"You have to understand, Aunt Maggie," Robert said to his aunt. "My atheism is just as important to me as your Christianity is to you."

Maggie's eyes went as wide as they had ever gone. The concept of atheism being important to anyone, of being anything more than just obstinate ignorance, of being an idea, a worldview, a thing someone would embrace with their whole being, their heart and mind was shocking to her. Even the devil was not an atheist, for the devil knew damn well (especially damn well) that there was a God.

Robert would never forget that look on Maggie's face. And over all the long years since, over all the family-gathering Christmases he was forced by his mother (even in his twenties) to attend where Maggie was always more than pleasant to him and always gave (from Herold and her) the best present he would receive each year, when he looked at her he saw *that face* replacing the kind and jolly family-loving Merry Christmas one that was actually there.

Elizabeth Porter (née Harper) was not only Robert's wife of fifteen years but was the head of the English Department at Pasadena City College. She was not looking forward to going to Uncle Herold's funeral service any more than Robert, she was always busy, and to take a day off would set her back in several classroom and administrative goals she had set. But she knew that if Robert did not attend the funeral, he would later regret it and would be annoyingly vocal about it off and on for years to come. To avoid having to listen to that was motivation enough to make sure Robert did not avoid the service, and for her to attend it as his loving wife.

Robert had tried to use the excuse that he was booked that same day so early in the morning at the SoCal Breakfast club so far away in Santa Monica and it would be rude to cancel this late, but Elizabeth wasn't having it.

"You go, and I'll be ready when you get back and we'll leave immediately. We may be a tad late, but we'll get there."

"Wouldn't it be more efficient for you to come with me to the Breakfast Club, then we'll leave directly from Santa Monica, go up PCH, and—"

"No way. For one thing, I've heard your speech many times. For another, if you think I can get ready that early in the morning to be presentable at the funeral, you have very little understanding of what a female has to go through to create a public face. We're not like you guys who just have to slip into your slacks one leg at a time, fasten your belts, run a comb through your hair if you have any, and tighten your tie, then off you go. You guys are a quick sketch, women are paintings."

"I think you abuse your poetic license."

"So sue me."

"It's going to be a hell of a lot of driving."

"You drive there. I'll drive back."

"You know I can't stand being a passenger."

"You'll recline the seat back and nap on the way home. You'll need it after waking up so ridiculously early."

"But—"

"Bob! He's *Your* Uncle Herold. He was the last connection to your mother, to some great childhood memories you have regaled me with for years."

"You want me to have closure."

"Well, as much as I hate that damn word, I guess, yes."

And so Robert was now on the 210 freeway almost ready to take the off ramp that would get him home to just—once Liz was comfortable in the car—turn around and get back on the freeway to travel the 150 miles to close out his history with his parent's generation.

Robert and Elizabeth, following the directions

Aunt Maggie had emailed them, got to the church in Lompoc after everyone had been seated, but before the actual service had started. It was not quite the little white clapboard church Robert had imagined with a spire on top of a bell tower. Rather it was a one-story brick complex with a day care and kindergarten attached. It did not have a bell tower, but a huge, tall cross that Robert immediately thought was sure to topple in the next earthquake, rose from the roof and reached (desperately?) to heaven. They found seats in the back of the sanctuary. As they were sitting, Robert noticed that Aunt Maggie, sitting up front, of course, was looking around and stopped when she spotted them. She signaled that they should come forward, but Robert signaled back that they were fine where they were. Then he saw his brother Richard, Dick to him and, most annoyingly, Dickie to all his colleagues at the Jet Propulsion Laboratory. He was sitting next to Aunt Maggie and pleaded with his eyes for Robert to join him and take on some of the burden. But Robert just smiled a not-so-sincere sorry.

There was appropriate music coming from the electronic organ being played by a dour looking middle-aged man who seemed to Robert to be a casting agent's dream for such a role. They had both been handed a program by a young woman when they entered, and it indicated that the dour looking man was the music and choir director of the church, a position that Maggie filled before her retirement. The program also included a longish quote from the New Testament which Robert did not bother to read, an nice photo of Uncle Herold (the same one enlarged and resting on an easel at the front by the pulpit), which Robert had never seen before, but thought was a very good one and he nudged Liz and asked her in a whisper to remind him to ask Aunt Maggie if he could get a copy of it.

Robert took a deep breath and tried to settle a certain feeling that was permeating his being. He almost shuddered. Liz asked how he was feeling, wondering if he was being hit by sadness and grief.

"No, just my normal, you know..."

"Oh yeah."

Churches creeped Robert out. It was as simple as that. These monuments to irrationality made his skin not just crawl but stampede in terror.

The service began when a man in a gray suit, just leaning into middle age, listed in the program as Reverand Stanley Davidson, ascended to the pulpit and greeted those gathered to bid a farewell to and celebrate the life of Herold Sullivan Fitch, a long-time member of their community and church, a loving husband and father, a friend to all. Robert was moved by the Reverand Davidson's words about his uncle, for they were heartfelt and it was obvious that he knew Herold well and had genuinely liked him. But then everyone liked Herold. At least Robert had never heard of anyone who didn't.

Then the Reverand's words left the sunlit hill of loving remembrance and descended into the dark forest of sermon. Suddenly he was telling those gathered—the mechanics and doctors and salesmen and housewives and school children and firefighters and pharmacists and store clerks and veterans of foreign wars and volunteers at charities and weekend athletes and amateur musicians and even a city councilmember—that they were all sinners. SINNERS! Born sinners, the sons and daughters of sinners, the parents of sinners, sinners all, all wallowing in sin, destined for the burning non-cleansing fires of Hell.

Robert didn't know whether to drop his jaw in shock or in preparation to guffaw. He and Elizabeth turned to each other and registered with their eyes their mutual secular-liberal-elitist, high-and-mighty, looking-down-their-noses-at-such-a-medieval-mindset reaction.

But then Reverand Davidson announced the "Good News." For those who have or will accept Jesus Christ as their Savior will be saved from the burning and will enter into the arms of God, into His realm in Heaven above where they will join the—

The what? The arms of Jesus? The Angels? The elect? No. They will join the party! For Heaven (according to Rev. Davidson) is an eternal party of joy and celebration, a fun party that delights with many delights and it will be delightful.

And then with a last reading from the bible, and the dour looking middle-aged man hitting the organ keys again, the service ended. The congregated rose their soar butts off the hard wooden pews, some clutching the program, some leaving them behind stuffed into the hymnal pockets in the back of the pew ahead of them, and filed out of their rows, some heading for the exits, some gathering about the family of the deceased to offer their condolences and words of support and quick mentions of the wonderfulness of Herold Sullivan Fitch.

Robert and Elizabeth beat a hasty retreat to the lobby of the church, wanting a further escape but knowing they needed to stand there to eventually receive Aunt Maggie and the cousins.

They had to wait many minutes, but eventually Maggie came up to Robert to accept the hug she knew was due her. She was a little woman for such a dynamic go-getter, and Robert had to bend down to give her a hug and quietly say what was required—he was so sorry; how was she doing; was there anything she needed? After the hug Maggie looking intensely into Robert's eyes with compassion for *his* lost and said, "I hope Reverand Stan's words gave you some consolation."

"Ah—" Robert was never good at equivocating. "Being told I was a sinner destined to burn in hell was not really designed to make me feel good, was it? Nor was being invited to an eternal party. I hate parties, always have. For that matter Uncle Herold also hated parties, as you well know."

Aunt Maggie's eyes of compassion quicky turned to eyes of pity. "You still think you are an atheist, don't you."

"I don't think it, Aunt Maggie. I just am."

"I've never understood this about you. I can't imagine the world, the universe, without God."

"You don't have to imagine it, it's all around you."

Aunt Maggie had no answer to that except to say, "It's just so sad. But you will come back to the house for something to eat."

"Well, we have a long drive home, and both Liz and I have busy days tomorrow."

"Ah come on Bob." Brother Richard had come up to them. "Never let it be said that the Brothers Porter skipped a good meal."

"Won't I be seeing you tomorrow at our weekly lunch?"

"You can never have too much of me, brother!"

It was a good meal. Aunt Maggie always provided a good meal. He caught up with his cousins, a male, a female, both working in retail, neither ever understanding what Robert did for a living except to peer into telescopes, which he was always doing as a child. Elizabeth talked with Maggie's much younger sister who was a high school teacher of English in

Fresno, and they traded book recommendations. They finally left much later than they should have.

Elizabeth was as good as her word and took the wheel for the long drive home. Robert did recline the passenger seat and semi-slept most of the way but heard the classical music Elizabeth had put on the radio, and the humming and whooshing of traffic unique to freeway travel. When Elizabeth left the 210 and descended onto surface streets, in the new relative quiet, Robert's memory went back to his childhood and semi-sleeping in the backseat of his dad's Toyota as they drove back at night after a day-long visit with relatives, sort of tracking the trip through sound, noting the stops, the goes, the turns, the speeding ups and slowing downs, and finally the familiar sounds and turns of their neighborhood streets ending with his dad pulling into their driveway. Although only semi-asleep, Robert would pretend to be dead asleep, forcing his dad to pick him up and carry him into the house and lovingly lay him on his bed with the *Star Trek* bedspread while cautioning brother Richard, who was always wide awake, to be quiet and not to wake up his brother. He would then undress Robert down to his underpants and tee-shirt and slip him between the sheets. When the light was turned off by his dad as he left the room, Robert would finally fall into a full sleep.

Robert and Richard's weekly brotherly lunch had become a tradition without them really noticing. Part of the ritual was to pick out a different restaurant each week somewhere in the Pasadena to South Pasadena area, although they could return to any restaurant they had been in before as long as it had not been the week before. This was necessary because there were only so many restaurants that met what the Brothers Porter considered their high standards. This week it was Mama Lu's Dumpling

House on Colorado in Old Town Pasadena.

"You know they don't call this area 'Old Town Pasadena' anymore," Dick said to Bob as he sat down to join him at a small table in the intimate space at Mama Lu's.

"They don't?" Bob said.

"Yeah, I just saw a sign. They just call it 'Old Pasadena' now."

"Not 'Old Town'?"

"Not 'Old Town'."

Robert thought about this for a moment. "It seems to me—"

"Yeah, me too."

"That 'Old Town Pasadena' has more charm to it, nostalgia even."

"Exactly. 'Old Pasadena' just sounds like a

doddering old man."

"Exactly."

Richard was only eighteen months younger than Robert, so they had been each other's playmates for years. They were also the beneficiaries of loving parents who had encouraged play and reading and thinking and questioning, not that either had needed much encouragement. There was never much sibling rivalry between them except maybe for a larger portion of the nightly dessert their mother served precisely at 8:30, usually ice cream but sometimes lovely silky smooth Jell-o pudding, usually chocolate but on occasion Richard's favorite, butterscotch. The most traumatic moments in their shared life were when Robert entered high school and Richard was still in middle school. And when Robert went away to college and Richard was still in high school.

Over their lunch of chive & pork dumplings Dick suddenly said, "I'm thinking of getting married."

"Really? Who to?"

"I haven't figured that out yet."

"Oh, you haven't?"

"No, I haven't."

"I was wondering because I didn't even know you were dating."

"I date!"

"I meant anyone in particular with any consistency."

"That's because I'm looking for a particular type."

"What type?"

"Short and dumpy."

"Short and dumpy?" Bob asked with a small measure of shock. "You've never dated a short and dumpy woman in your life."

"Well, that's what I'm looking for now."

There was some silence between the two brothers as they both dipped a chive and pork dumpling into soy sauce and ingested them.

Then Robert said, "I'm waiting for the revelation as to exactly why you now want to marry a short and dumpy woman."

"Because I want to give her the nickname of "my little pork dumpling.""

Richard kept a stoneface as he refused to acknowledge that he had been set up. "I suggest you get an airtight prenup."

Just as stone-faced, Dick said, "Yeah I'll do that."

But both brothers were smiling inside.

It was debatable which brother was the smarter one. They both excelled at math and all science classes, they both liked history, tolerated P.E., but only Robert pulled As in English and literature. He loved novels of all genres. Richard could only read the cliff notes of classics and nodded off reading those. But Richard had a closer relationship with nature, plants and animals. Robert considered nature to be a nuisance and filled to capacity with bugs and would have been happy to live his whole life indoors. Air was only fresh to him if it came through a ventilating system. But the real difference between the two brothers who in so many other ways were alike, was a difference of vision. Robert wanted to see far into the past and the future of the universe. Richard was happy to take in the view of the present, the here and now, extending his vision only to the confines of our solar-centered system of space.

And so Richard became a space flight engineer at JPL, guiding probes around the solar system. And Robert became a cosmologist at Caltech, looking long ago and far away.

Robert and Richard left Mama Lu's Dumpling House and began to walk along Colorado Boulevard, heading towards the parking structure they had both parked at, when Robert suddenly stopped.

"What's that?" Robert exclaimed with some confusion and a modicum of alarm.

Richard, now two steps ahead turned around and took two steps back to Robert as mid-day foot traffic passed them in both directions. "What's what?" he asked Richard.

"That!" Robert pointed directly ahead of him at—to Richard—seemingly nothing out of the ordinary that would merit Robert's query and pointing.

But to Robert there hung in the air six yards in front of him and twelve feet above him a small bright spot, perfectly white, brilliantly shining, not a reflection of something somewhere else, but the primary source. Robert blinked instinctually, then again, but the bright spot remained.

Following Robert's pointed finger, Richard looked and saw nothing. As, obviously, did everyone else on the sidewalk walking east or west. He looked back to his brother and saw in his face an aspect of wonder mixed horror that he had never seen before. "Robert?"

Robert did not hear his brothers concern. He became unaware of the moving points of humanity around him. He could only stare at the small bright shining spot of white light. Then it expanded, expanded quickly until, to Robert, all was white, pure bright white, eye-burning white.

Then all was black.

"Robert! Robert!" Richard yelled out as Robert

collapsed onto the sidewalk.

2

911 was called, an ambulance arrived with siren blaring, people all along this section of Colorado stopped to stare, because how could one not. Richard was on the ground supporting his brother's head. He had felt for a pulse. It was strong. He had checked Robert's breathing. It was steady and seemed to him normal. Dick called to Bob over and over to no response. Then a EMT from the ambulance made a welcomed intrusion and took over. Soon Robert was lifted onto a wheeled gurney, then installed inside the

ambulance. Richard joined him and rode with him to Huntington Hospital, to Emergency.

The black was solid, a deep ebony of negation, excluding everything that was anything, a something of nothing, a total absence of any presence.

And yet—there was sound. Someone was breathing nearby, a magazine page was turned, footsteps went by, a wheel squeaked as it rolled along, voices were making statements, asking questions, far off a laughed laugh, a woman cried out for a nurse with pain propelling the cry.

Then, the black seemed less black, seemed filled with—with what? Agitated specks of—of gray?

The curtains of his eyelids rose. White walls. A beeping. A man stood quickly, the magazine that was on his lap slid off and slapped the floor.

"Hey, Bob! Bob? Are you back with us?" Richard had come close, looked down upon Robert.

"You're—you're my brother," Robert stated to Richard.

Richard chuckled. "That's right. Unless mother lied to us. But Dad always said we could trust her."

"Bob!"

It was a female voice of some familiarity.

Elizabeth set down the two paper cups of coffee she had gone to get, and came over to the bed, on the opposite side from Richard. "Honey, how do you feel?"

Robert looked up at the female face hovering over him and raised his head sightly towards her. "Is?"

"Is what?"

"Liz?"

"Yes, it's me, your wife."

Robert lowered his head into the cradle of a fat pillow and starred up at the industrial type ceiling. "Met—first time—saw you on the steps of the—the library at—university."

"Yes, yes, that's right Bob. How nice of you to remember," Elizabeth said with a small, delighted laugh.

"So—so academic—in a beautiful way."

"What?"

"So—so beautiful—in an academic way."

"Bob?"

"Hello! Excuse me."

A man entered the room. A doctor by the

name of Souferzade, as the stitching on his white coat announced. But he did not rely on that for an introduction.

"I'm Dr. Souferzade, but you can call me Dr Soufer. I'm a neurologist that your primary doctor called in to take a look at you."

Elizabeth and Richard greeted the doctor and Robert just stared at him.

"I'm happy to see you are awake again."

"He was awake before?" Richard asked.

"Yes, they tell me he regained consciousness in the emergency room, told everyone that it was his birthday, then became unconscious again."

"Today's not his birthday. It's not even close to it," Elizabeth said.

"Well that's interesting. Here, let me have a look."

Elizabeth and Richard parted from the hospital bed allowing Dr. Soufer access to the patient. He did his checking, looking, peering, feeling, and listening, as doctors are wont to do.

"Well," the doctor said as he finished. "Everything seems right and regular, which goes along with what we found out from the CT Scans and other tests."

"Which is?" Elizabeth asked.

"That everything is absolutely as it should be. There is no evidence of a stroke or any damage to the brain. His heart is healthy. The emergency doctor noted that his pulse was good when he came in, and that his breathing was normal and steady. And he responded to stimuli. Essentially, he was asleep and not in a coma-like unconscious. A deep sleep but, still, nothing of concern. Now the admitting doctor said it was reported that he complained of a bright light in front of him."

"That's right," Richard said. "But I wouldn't say complained. It was more of a simple statement and wondering what the hell it was."

"And he seemed to experience no pain."

"No, nothing like that."

"And you saw no light."

"No, nothing. And nobody else on the street seemed to, as well."

"Well, we seem to have a medical mystery here. At the moment, he seems perfectly fine, but I would like to keep him overnight for observation, just to make sure."

Robert, who had said nothing during this time, now said, "Doctor?"

"Yes, Mr. Porter."

"Actually, he's a doctor too," Richard unnecessarily said.

"Oh?"

"Doctor of Cosmology."

"Oh, yes, someone said he was from Caltech."

"Is it my turn now?" Robert propped himself us a little in bed.

"Sure big brother," Richard said, feeling the relief.

"Doctor, when and where did you get your medical degree?"

Elizabeth, Richard, and Dr. Souferzade were all taken aback by the bluntness of Robert's question, which Robert quickly perceived, and so he quickly said, "I'm not questioning your skills, Doctor, I'm just curious."

"Well, I got my degree from John Hopkins in 1995."

"Were your parents proud of you."

"I would say so, yes."

"Were you married at the time."

"No. Nor am I now."

"Do you remember the weather on that day."

"Honey, what the—"

"It was raining, hard. And it was very cold. It was mid-December."

"You remember that very well."

"We tend to remember significant days. Now, despite the clean bill of health I've given you. I think you should rest. I will check in on you before you are discharged tomorrow."

"Thank you," patient, wife and brother all said.

"What was that all about, Bob?" Elizabeth asked.

"What?"

"Giving the doctor the third degree," Richard answered.

"Nothing. Really, nothing."

But Robert was lying. Not completely, he was curious, but it was really a test. A test that the doctor had failed. Because Robert knew that Dr. Souferzade could not have gotten his medical degree in 1995 because there never really was a 1995. For the universe didn't exist then. The universe, Robert now knew for a fact, didn't exist until earlier that day, precisely at what every person in the greater Los Angeles area would have considered to be 1:17 PM on this Tuesday April 22 in the year 2025, but was actually second one of hour one of day one of week one of month one of year one of the existence of the universe. Robert had no doubt of that fact. In fact he had total faith that it was true.

3

Turtles and olive trees.

It was the Monday after Robert's short hospital stay. He had taken the rest of the week off, although the doctor had said there was no reason why he couldn't return to work immediately. But Robert said no to himself and Elizabeth and Richard.

"I don't feel—how do I say this—um—I don't feel one hundred percent myself. Does that make sense?"

"Well," Richard said sitting in Robert and Elizabeth's spacious living room, well-designed with tasteful furniture, and never cluttered with the day-to-day detritus of two *Homo sapiens* living their lives together. "Despite the doc's clean bill of health, you have suffered a traumatic, uh, thing, you know. You're bound to be—I don't know—exhausted, I guess."

"I don't feel exhausted. I just don't feel myself."

"Whose 'self' do you feel?" Elizabeth said as she entered the room carrying her briefcase.

"Well, that's the question. I don't know. Just not myself. And until I do, I would prefer some time away from work. The universe, I guess, can carry on without me for a few days."

"I wish I could say that the PCC English Department can carry on for a few days without me, but, still, if you would like me to stay with you..."

"No, that's okay. Actually, I think some time alone is what I need."

"So you want to get rid of me also?"

"I'll never be rid of you, Brother. Thank goodness. But for now..."

"Understood. Just as well, the Hercules probe won't fly itself, so I better get back to JPL."

Robert wasn't sure he ever got back to feeling like himself. Or maybe he did and he just didn't fully recognize himself. But, in any case, he was back now on the Caltech campus, walking among the many olive trees that shaded the academics, and, at the moment, staring at the many turtles who resided in the pools of the Troop Memorial Garden. Hard-shelled funny looking creatures.

What must the four directly beneath him in his view think of his looming presence. Two raised their heads and seemed to look at him, but he knew they were thinking nothing of him. Can they even see me? No, even if they can see me, the cool of the water, the warmth of the sun, the food they ingest, that's all they probably think about in their little universe. That and the occasional fuck to keep populating the pools. Of me they think nothing. To them I am nothing. To them I don't exist. But the question is—do I exist to me?

Such philosophy! Coming from a hard-headed (hard-hearted?), hard-shelled scientist such as myself. And why am I here? Not universally here. But here-here, on this spot. Here by the turtle pools contemplating the awareness of hard-shelled reptiles. Robert had parked his car, as he always did, in the underground parking for the Cahill Center for Astronomy and Astrophysics at the south end of the campus where his office was. But instead of entering the building and quickly walking to his office, greeting whoever was in the halls to greet, he crossed California Boulevard and entered the main part of the small campus and walked through out all of it, stopping at each building, the old ones and the relatively new ones. The names on the buildings he stated out loud as he passed them: Athenaeum, Firestone, Guggenheim, Beckman, Baxter, Bechtel, Mudd, Broad, Fleming, and on and on. He had been a cosmologist at Caltech for more that twelve years, passing these named buildings countless of times. He must have mentioned their names many times, giving directions to visitors, or telling someone where a particular science was studied and performed. And yet, now, today, these many minutes of his walking tour of the small campus, he was convinced that he was enunciating their names, flowing them out of his mouth, for the very first time ever in the whole history of the universe—

which comprised just a week.

He stopped when he came to the Troop Memorial Garden and its turtles in the pools there. It was a spot he rarely stopped at and usually barely noticed if he passed it, his mind often on billions of years ago or a quintillion miles away. But right now, today, this moment, he realized that it had been his destination. For it was turtles he wanted.

"Maybe the Earth does rest on the back of a turtle," he quietly said to himself.

It was a sweet contemplation, but a useless one. I should get to work, Robert thought and left the pools and quickly got himself to the nearby California Boulevard and crossed it get to the three story, terra-cotta-colored-panels-covered Cahill building. It was an imposing and almost intimidating three-story building with one corner jutting out like the pointed bow of a dangerous ship or the proud chin of arrogant man. It was a rectangle building, but not a perfect rectangle, as if it was made from building blocks by a five-year-old.

Robert entered and felt comfortable in the familiar surroundings he knew so well and yet knew that he had never set foot in this building before. He was sure of that fact.

It was a strange interior for such an imposing exterior, comprising narrow corridors and small offices, which Robert had always (or had he?) seen as ironic for the daily view of the few big brains that occupied these places was of a vast expanding universe, so large most people couldn't contemplate it, and even these men and women whose professional task it was to contemplate it sometimes admitted that the concept of its size also blew them away. And yet if you walked down the corridor, you often saw the individual occupants of individual small offices hunkering down, looking down, scribbling on papers, reading papers, viewing computer screens, often on small laptops, focused on such small slices of their immediate realities.

The corridors would have seemed oppressive if it wasn't that they had no finished ceilings, say twelve feet above the floor, but rather, all the heating pipes, light fixtures, electrical wiring, and air conduits were exposed in the upper atmosphere of the corridor, giving the place a very industrial feel. Robert had noticed that this seemed to be an architectural conceit here in Pasadena because he had noticed that several restaurants along Colorado had the same no-ceiling, exposed-airy-guts design—

But wait—

Was it sheep-like architects following suit? Or was it a glitch, a glitch in the creation of this fully formed universe created last Tuesday on April 22 at 1:17 PM? A glitch that just didn't fill in the ceilings like a five-year-old not filling in all the spaces in a coloring book.

A glitch.

Like—

Me. Knowing the truth of the true creation of this fully formed universe when all others are accepting the standard model I have accepted for years that really didn't exist because existence wasn't really there before April—

"Uh!" Robert clutched his head and bent forward almost in a collapse.

"Doctor Porter!"

Sean Chen, a graduate student in astrophysics, who assisted Robert, ran from one end of the ground floor corridor to catch and clutch Robert before he could fall, and brought him up straight. "Are you okay?"

"What? Oh, Sean. Yes, I'm—I'm fine now. Just a sudden headache. Whew, wow, that was something."

"We heard you were ill. Shouldn't you go home?"

"No. It's gone now." Robert took a deep breath in and let it out slowly. "Yes. It's all gone. But—but why don't you walk me to my office."

"Sure. Happy to."

Robert's office was on the third floor, which they ascended to via the elevator. Usually Robert took the stairs in his ongoing effort to keep fit, but he did not protest when Sean guided him to the elevator. Robert was happy to sit in his chair and breathe some long breaths in and out.

"Can you do me a favor, Sean?"

"Of course."

"Can you run over to Browne and get me a bottle of water."

"Sure.'

"Let me give you some money."

"Forget it. My treat," Sean said as he quickly left for the Browne Dining Hall.

"What the hell," Robert said to himself as he leaned back in his chair and took in the view of the large, framed photo he had put on his wall just a few months ago (assuming there was a few months ago). It was the first direct image of another planetary system located about 300 light-years away around a star like our Sun. The star burned brightly in the center of the picture, maybe six planets reflecting the sun's light were spotted here and there, unless one or two were actually other stars farther away, but bright enough to be seen. The picture had been captured by one of the ESO telescopes in Chile. It had always been a dream of Robert's, an eyeball view of a distant planetary system. Not just twinkle-twinkle little stars in our sky, not just the pinpoints of light that did not twinkle that were our neighbor planets, but a view of another—or *an other*—planetary system like ours but maybe nothing like ours. Mysteries of the Universe. The drive that had compelled him the whole of his adult life.

Or not.

Was it a joke?

Was all of it a cosmic joke?

His head started to hurt again, but Robert took a deep breath and told it not to. Where was that—

"Water, Doc." Sean entered with a frosty flimsy bottle of water. Robert grabbed it, unscrewed the little cap, and began to drink, swallow after swallow after swallow until the bottle was collapsed.

Sean with wide eyes said, "I guess you were thirsty."

Robert caught his breath, then said, "I hate these new flimsy bottles." He tossed it with great disdain into his trash can. "But they do kind of remind you how flimsy we are. Thin skin bags of mostly water. Not to get too philosophical about it."

"But you're feeling better now, right?"

"Much, yes, thank you. But do me a favor, check in on me in a couple of hours?"

"Of course, Doc. I'll be glad to."

After Sean left, Robert leaned back in his chair and looked again at the ESO pic of the 300-light-years-away planetary system. High-tech star gazing.

Robert's mind massaged a memory of Robert and Richard (or Bobby and Ricky, as their parents called them) star gazing in the most low-tech way—via their naked eyes. Laying on a blanket laid on the grass of their childhood front lawn in a small town on the edge of a desert in Nevada. They traveled the arm of the Milky Way and took their eyes off-road to look at stars scattered throughout their galaxy. They counted the shooting stars they saw and keep a record of how many each night in a little spiral notebook. They noted which non-twinkling planets were visible each night and entered that as well in their little spiral notebook. The moon, of course, an always welcomed visitor in all its phases, they loved to gaze at. But it was the full moon they loved the best.

They challenged each other to really "feel" outer space, they challenged each other to mind-trip beyond Earth to move among the stars and tell of their trips. Ricky's tellings were of their own planets and the satellites orbiting around them, he loved the thought of visiting them in the future, he loved the thought of the future, he loved science fiction in books and on TV and films that took him to those planets and moons. Bobby thought of the past, of where this all came from, he wanted to witness the creation and the expansion of space through time to now, right here, right now. Ricky was a homebody. Bobby was a wanderer in space and time.

But it was all ethereal mental pleasure cruises, fun and blood-exciting but not really real. Until their parents bought them for Christmas two matching telescopes, one white, one black. One might have been enough, lessons in sharing are always good for young boys, but their dad was a bright guy and knew that his boys had two different views to focus in on. Why set up a fight? Let them share not one telescope, but two views, and the different illuminations they provided. So the brothers would position their telescopes on the front lawn. Ricky would aim his not only and obviously at the moon when it was in the sky, and any planet available overhead. And Bobby would aim his at the depths of the Milky Way's visible arm and more vacant spots of the sky, time-tripping to other galaxies and stars calling to him from before.

Robert walked his mind among this memory and smiled. And where were the brothers today? Still both in their separate corners, both illuminating the other with mutual gratitude.

So how can—damn it! How can I now know what I know that it's all a lie, loving my childhood, my brother, my father for being so astute about his boys. Memories handed to me by some phenomenon, by some cosmic quirk. By some entity? Seeming so real yet flimsy like that damn crinkly water bottle you can't really get a good grip on.

Robert pinched himself.

He pinched a fold of flesh on his arm and applied as much pressure as a finger cooperating with a thumb could provide.

It was an age-old test of reality.

And it hurt.

I'm alive. I'm real. I'm here. But that really wasn't the question, was it? The question is how long I've been alive, real, here. Just about a week, just like everybody else, everything else, he believed.

Believed. Deeply. For he knew. He had the knowledge, not just the thought, not just a mind experiment. He *knew*. And he had faith in the knowledge.

His headache returned. He felt as if he was going to faint again. But he opened his computer and read his emails of which there were many and let his focus on them pull him back into clear consciousness.

4

Robert made it through the rest of the day with just a hint of the headache making itself known. He did some calculations. He talked to a friend at NASA, he talked to a friend at the European Space Agency, he ate the lunch he had packed for himself. It was a cream cheese and black olive sandwich.

Why had he made himself a cream cheese and black olive sandwich? He had not had one for years. His mom used to make them. Especially when they had moved to California and were on a family road trip to go camping, his parents both loved camping. They would leave well before dawn on the first day of his father's two-week vacation, and head north on the I-5. His mother had prepared the car by padding the floor of the back seat into a bed where Ricky would sleep, while Bobby stretched out on the back seat, a blanket tucked around him. Dad would head towards the I-5 and would be on it as the sun rose, and in the midst of waking Bobby could hear his parents talking quietly, expressing subtle awe for the sunrise. He would pull himself up to a sitting position and his mother would tell him to go back to sleep and he would say, "I want to see," meaning see the sunrise. "Okay," his mother said and he would take a good look and think it was the greatest thing he had ever seen, and he would ask "How does the sun move?" And his father, his eyes still on the long ribbon in front of him would answer. "It doesn't, Bobby, it's the Earth that's moving or rather rotating, like a merry-go-round. So it only looks like the sun is moving. It's an illusion." "Oh," Bobby would say trying to imagine it, to see it, to fathom it. Then he would lay back down on the back seat and fall asleep again. A little later both he and Ricky would be woken and find the car no longer moving but parked at a ranch restaurant where they would get breakfast. The boys were in their PJs, but their mother did not make them get dressed, just put on the robes they had, and the new, warm, fuzzy-inside slippers she had bought them just a week before. As they walked to the restaurant, the boys would be impressed by several huge trucks parked off to the side. Inside they were taken to a booth by a motherly waitress of vast experience, who handed a picture to color and some crayons to the boys. Then it was pancakes with loads of syrup and bacon and a tall, cold glass of milk. Back on the road it was boring to look out at the ongoing landscape of agricultural California, a scene of no interest to them, but mother, always prepared, had bought both boys 10 comic books each, and they read them greedily and lost themselves in humor and super-powered adventures. At lunch time, father pulled into a pull-over stop that had restrooms and a little park with picnic tables. The boys ran to the restrooms and mother laid a plastic tablecloth on one of the picnic tables and laid out their lunch. Cream cheese and black olive sandwiches for her and the boys, and a ham sandwich for their father. And little bags of chips. And an apple each.

Bobby loved his cream cheese and black olive sandwich. In all of his childhood, nothing had ever tasted so great. Not even birthday cake or hot dogs or macaroni and cheese, or the peach cobbler his mother made with peaches from their own backyard peach trees. His mother only made this sandwich when they were on a road trip to some campground to sleep in a big tent in flannel-lined sleeping bags. So they were the very definition of something special, of a rare treat, a taste to look forward to with the tickle of saliva gathering in your mouth, and to look back on with anticipation for a future taste of this ambrosia between two slices of Wonder Bread.

Was this why Robert had made himself a cream cheese and black olive sandwich? Because the memory had come back to him that morning so strong and clear, with his parents' quiet voices, a music of contentment, residing in his head making him dizzy, and not the kind of dizzy that makes you fall, but the kind of dizzy that makes you giddy. So he got out the bread—not Wonder Bread but his favorite sourdough, and the cream cheese stored in the refrigerator, waiting for Sunday morning bagels, and opened a can of black olives, and made himself a fat-with-cream cheese and black olives sandwich, which he almost ate for breakfast, but didn't because that would have cheated him of the anticipation.

Robert could have taken his sandwich to Browne Dinning Hall, to get a hot cup of tea and sit to eat his lunch, but he couldn't wait. When he got hungry around 12:30, he opened his briefcase, retrieved the sandwich, quickly extricated it from the plastic baggie, laid out a napkin on his desk and took a bite of the sandwich. It—was—explosive in recall of childhood delight. Was this the past, the past incarnate? The past he knew for certain didn't really happen. But if not, what the hell? Why the fuck? He took another bite. It was exactly as he remembered it.

Exactly.

But how could he remember what never was?

His headache was beginning again.

He took three Ibuprofin tablets from a bottle he kept in his desk and swallowed them dry.

He closed his eyes. He groped for his sandwich siting on the laid-out napkin on his desk. He found it and brought it to his mouth and slowly consumed it, payingclose attention to taste and texture.

Real. So real in his mouth. The past. He so much wanted to swallow the past.

90

5

Just before leaving for the day Liz called to remind him that she would not be home until late. She had promised the head of the Drama Department that she would attend a production of three student plays. So the house was empty, a furnished vacuum with the oppressive quiet of the absence of love. Or not love itself, but the object of love. Or companionship—emotional, intellectual, trivial.

Robert moved directly to their bedroom and got out of his clothes and put on sweatpants and a tee-shirt with the famous picture of Albert Einstein sticking out his tongue on it, a gift from his brother.

He slipped on slippers and cat-footed it into the den-study he shared with Liz, a book-lined room with two desks, two fat comfy chairs with side tables, and a rectangle large screen TV. Robert plopped himself onto the comfy chair designated his, and concentrated on breathing, just breathing, and hopefully not thinking. But it was to no avail, thinking was much of what he had always done.

1:17 PM this last Tuesday on the 22nd day in this month of April in this year of 2025, he thought. *The beginning of the universe, the beginning of time.* The truth of this was as obvious to him as the little brown mole on the back of his left hand between his thumb and forefinger which had been there for as long as he could remember.

His head began to ache again, but only slightly.

To remember. It was such the marvelous mark of being human. Not just existing in the moment, but existing in an existence that stretched behind, a trail of personal history traveling within hailing distance of others like you, acquaintances and strangers, famous people governing you and entertaining you, lovers and haters, the exciting and the mundane. And animals, your pets, other people's pets, horses on parade, cattle giving of themselves to feed you, not to mention pigs, and birds, oh so many birds, flying high, singing sweetly or seeming to scream in protest. Buildings, structures, abodes offering shelter and warmth. Conveyances, cars, buses, choo-choos. Choo-choos? No, trains, locomotives, steam engines. How clever we are to have so many names. Names help us remember, give our memories stakes to tie themselves down with.

Is it, I think, therefore I am? Or, I remember, therefore I am? But if the memories be false, am I not?

Robert began to wish he was not a teetotaler.

He looked over to the bottom shelf of one of their bookcases. It was lined with photo albums. He got up out of his comfy chair and retrieved one of the albums, an old one, one he had before he met and married Liz. Most of the photos were taken when he was a doctoral candidate at MIT and a teaching assistant to the renown, TV savvy cosmologist Dr. Cleaveland Jordan, often seen on talk shows and PBS documentaries, including his own, *Wonders of the Universe*, which showed off not only the sharpness of his mind, but the handsomeness of his face. He was also the author of many books on his subject, and one memoir, *To Dance Among the Stars*. He was almost an American institution. But he was also a subtly arrogant bastard, wonderfully charming in front of a camera, be it motion or still, or an audience, but a bit petulant when only surrounded by staff and assistants. But Robert loved him. He grew up watching him on TV, knocked down delightfully by the revelations of the universal wonders shown and explained, but, most importantly, conveyed with a wide-eyed enthusiasm by this person of authority in the matter. To be such a person of authority in a chosen matter. Was there any other goal as great as that?

Robert sat back into his comfy chair and opened the photo album. Ah, yes! Many photos of campus life, fun times, silly doings, visits back home, and Liz, there's Liz. So young, so attractive. Funny, Robert never thought that Elizabeth Harper was beautiful or even pretty, for she was neither. But she was damn attractive. She had an intellectual charisma that was undeniable. She was a Literature major, with a concentration on world literature. Robert was not a reader of novels, not even science fiction. But when Liz began to talk about a book, breaking it down to the parts that made the whole that moved her so deeply, he listened with a sense of awe and stared at her in her usually baggy clothes that hid any hint of a blood-fed fleshy body beneath.

"Why are you studying literature at MIT?" he asked her soon after they met.

"I like being surrounded by nerds.'

"Oh."

"You know, all you science and engineering geeks who are shy around women, especially pretty women. And since I am not a pretty woman—"

"Oh, I don't—"

"Don't contradict me."

"Oh, okay."

Liz began again. "Since I am not a pretty woman, I figured the men here would not be shy around me and that could foster some fine male companionships for me."

"You like men?"

"I like sex. And since my leanings are towards heterosexual sex, then, yes, obviously, I like men."

"What—uh, what kind of men do you like?"

"Your type."

"Oh."

"So why don't you ask me out?"

Robert's brain quickly searched dating scenarios trying to come up with something unique, but could only come up with, "A movie?"

"Sure, I like movies. But why don't we start with dinner and drinks."

When Liz shed her baggy clothes their first night of sex, Robert was delighted to see that she had a beautifully formed body, wonderfully smooth skin, and breasts just the right size to be alluring and not disappointing or, worse, grossly in your face.

Robert became giddy again, almost reeling, and a bit dizzy with a very happy state looking at these pics of bits of captured light that seemingly proved his past existence. And he so much—so much wanted to believe they were true but—damn it!

He almost—almost slammed the album shut, but, no, one page more, maybe two, of the lies, the falsehoods, somehow made into images of things that never happened.

How the hell could he believe that!

His headache grew sharper. So he stopped the anger that was building up. He concentrated on breathing slowly, and then slowly turned one more leaf of the album.

Ah! Him at Picadilly Circus, London.

He had been asked by Dr. Jordan to accompany him on a book tour to the UK. Dr. Johnson portrayed it as a learning experience for Robert, learning the ins and outs of taking science to the masses. But Robert wasn't that naïve, he knew that Jordan just wanted him to be his dogsbody. But that was perfectly fine by Robert—it was still a trip to the UK, and especially London.

It was his mother's fault. He spent many years of his childhood watching old British movies with her on their TV. His mother was a dedicated anglophile, reading mainly British mysteries, and British travel books, and loving any film that took place in England, especially WWII movies of keeping calm and carrying on. Robert later developed his own love for British TV, when many began broadcasting and cabling in America. So to travel to the reality of so many beloved filmed locations was an exciting prospect for him. He happily accepted Dr. Jordan's invitation and spent 10 days following him around England, Wales and Scotland, taking care of his needs as he was a guest on radio and TV chat shows, and appeared at bookstores for signing events, and one riverside literary festival, and fulfilling all requests that Dr. Jordan had. The BBC, which had broadcast all of his TV documentaries, gave Dr. Jordan a fine reception at Broadcasting House at Langham Place the night before his departure, which Robert greatly enjoyed as he got to meet some BBC stars he had watched for years.

The next morning Robert made sure Dr. Jordan got into a black taxi in time to make his flight out of Heathrow. But Robert was going to stay a few more days. Dr. Jordan had paid for his hotel room for the rest of the week and gave him the balance of the Travelers Checks that his publisher had provided. "Enjoy yourself," he said with a smile, a kind smile. Robert was greatly moved.

So, later that day he found himself walking all around London, travel bag slung over his shoulder, passing and stopping to look at history, architecture, rushing humanity, large green parks, fast moving taxis, big red buses, lots of bike riders, shops small and large, a whole row of bookshops, each of which he popped in, looking at but not buying books which would amount to heavy tomes to carry, and a heavy drain on the traveler's checks. But he did buy several light-weight antique prints from stacks of pages torn from old books, that were a specialty of these shops. He brought two by Hogarth, one a scene from the life of Henry the Eighth, the other a scene from *Don Quixote*. He bought a weird one by Doré of some huge, snake-like monster in a forbidding landscape. And another picturing a 19th century westward looking view of The Canongate section of Edinburgh, which he and Dr. Jordan had visited just three days before. He remembered them all, could see them clearly, of course he could, for there they were on the south wall of the den, so long ago lovingly framed.

He ended that day's trek in Picadilly Circus, that great roundabout centered by the Shaftsbury Memorial Fountain topped by the statue of, no, not Eros as most believe, but of Anteros, the god of requited love, which must have been a satisfying god to be. Robert was standing on the stepped platform of the fountain, along with many others, many sitting on the steps, when a young man with a camera approached him. He explained that he worked for the Japanese Fuji Film company, always ready to compete with Kodak, and he's taking pictures of tourists in London with the big, FUJI FILM sign crowed among all the other giant neon product signs, like COCA COLA and SANYO mounted on the rounded corner building on the North side.

"How did you know I was a tourist?" Robert asked.

"I don't know, mate. You can just tell."

Robert was willing to have his picture taken, why not? Click! Click! Two shots from two different angles, both of which included the fountain in the background. The young man thanked him and then mention that if Robert would like copies of the pics, he would be happy to mail them to him for the price of a certain not insignificant number of British pounds sterling. Robert mention that he lived in

America, but that did not seem to faze the photographer. Robert thought quickly. This could certainly be a scam, but—but he really would love to have the pictures. He gave the young man his address in America and parted with the pounds and tried to be happy about it as he walked back to his hotel.

This was in early April. After Robert returned home, he waited for weeks for the mailman to deliver his photos, but none came. It didn't take much to convince him that he had been scammed and he hated the idea that he, soon to be a Ph.D., could be taken in this way. Vanity—he blamed it on vanity. He felt like shit. Then, on his 30th birthday in late May, the photos arrived! And they were fine. Ah! Here was the learning experience.

Robert remembered all this. He remembered it is some detail, but not all details, he was sure. But that's the way memory works. Or—or maybe memory works this way because all memories are false memories because how could they be anything else but given the fact—yes! Damn it! The fact! Given the fact, as he knew it so well, that there was nothing, nothing at all, no Picadilly Circus, no antique prints, no Fuji, no disappointment, no elation when the disappoint proved false, no England, no English movies, no Mom and me watching those movies, no Dr. Jordan, now long dead, but not dead because he never was alive, no photo album before 1:17 PM on Tuesday April 22 in this year called 2025 but really was year 1.

Year One.

With his head now pounding, Dr. Robert Porter fainted in his comfy chair. The photo album fell off his lap and slapped onto the hardwood floor.

6

"Bob?"

Robert did not respond to Elizabeth's probing question. He was deeply asleep in his chair, breathing smoothly. She had gotten home a little after eleven and had found him in their den, asleep in his chair. Which worried her. Robert never fell asleep in his chair.

She shook him gently, "Robert?" There was still no response. So with a concerned and sharp "Honey!" she shook him not so gently.

Robert awoke, opening his eyes to his wife's face. "When was the first time we fucked?" He asked her in a clear, commanding voice, not a sleep-groggy one.

"What?"

"The first time we did it. You know, had sex. I think I remember, but I want you to confirm it."

Elizabeth picked up the photo album from the floor and placed it on his side table, saying, "What kind of dream were you having?"

"I wasn't dreaming at all, I don't think. I just woke up with that question on my mind."

"Well, that's, sort of, you know, weird."

"But, what's your answer?"

"You seriously want to know?"

"I do."

"I don't know, specifically," she said as she moved over to her comfy chair and sat. "Sometime during college, certainly."

"It was on October 16th around five-thirty in the afternoon. We each skipped a class. We were, at first, only going to perform mutual masturbation, because for some strange reason you were not on The Pill, but then, after that, and after cleaning up we laid back down in bed, still nude, to, you know, cuddle, and, you know, nature kind of took its course."

"You remember all that?"

"I'm surprised you don't."

"Well, you've always been more the romantic than me."

"And you, a literature professor."

"I do remember where it happened."

"My off-campus apartment."

"Yes, because, I wouldn't do it in my dorm room."

"Your roommate Kristine did!"

"That's probably why I didn't want to. Kristine was a slut."

"Whatever happened to her?"

"She became a lawyer. She's made a fortune representing women accusing men of sexual abuse."

"Do you think it all really happened?"

"What?"

"Sex. College. Dorm rooms. Slutty roommates. Did it really all happen, or do we just remember it? And what is memory anyway? Just neurons firing in our brains looking for something to do. How do we know we can trust them?"

"Robert! What—" She knew there was too much panic in her voice, so she stopped, thought, took in a deep breath, and began again. "What is wrong? How's your head, does it still hurt?"

"Off and on."

"You should go see the doctor tomorrow."

"I'm suddenly feeling very tired. And hungry."

"Did you have any dinner?"

"I don't think so."

"Well, there you go." Elizabeth stood, satisfied with the mundaneness of her husband's problem. "I'll scramble you some eggs."

"Do I like eggs?" Robert stood, preparing to follow Elizabeth toward food.

"What? Of course you like eggs, you've always liked eggs."

"Really, that's odd, that's very odd. Because I've never had eggs before."

"Bob—I'm getting worried."

"No, seriously. I would swear on a stack of bibles I don't believe in that I have never, ever, in my short existence, consumed any eggs. Despite knowing what eggs are. Despite having a memory of eating eggs. Despite having a clear memory of their taste."

Elizabeth looked at her husband feeling confused and fearful and angry that this was happening. "Bob, something serious is happening. We've got to get you to the hospital first thing in the morning."

"Sure, sure, why not?" Robert said almost gayly. "But first scrambled eggs, right?"

"Yes, scramble eggs first."

As they headed toward the kitchen, Robert said, "My mother used to eat scrambled eggs and cow brains."

Elisabeth, assuming this was a joke, went along with it. "Really?"

"Yes, really, she did. But then, of course, you understand, she really never did. Because there were no cows before 1:17 PM on Tuesday April 22 in this year called 2025."

7

The next morning Robert refused to go to the hospital. "I'm feeling fine, Liz," he said to Elizabeth as they stood in the kitchen chatting, each eating oatmeal out of special bowls with handles a friend of Elizabeth's had made.

"Really?" Elizabeth looked for any sign that her husband was fibbing. But he looked sincere.

"Really. Besides I'm having lunch today with Richard."

"You are? I thought it was going to be Thursday this week."

"I called him and changed it."

"You did? When?" Elizabeth finished her oatmeal and placed the bowl in the sink, running some water into it.

"At three-o-clock this morning."

"Oh, he must have loved you for that!"

"He was a bit grumpy about it."

"I'll bet. Well, if you really think you're feeling okay..."

"I am, I'm feeling my oats! Literally," he said as he indicated his bowl, now empty of oatmeal, "and figuratively." He placed his bowl in the sink and did as Elizabeth had, filling it with water, knowing that Maria, their daily house cleaner would soon be there to wash them up.

They left the house together and the driveway separately in two cars.

Alone in the cocoon of his car, Robert took a moment to measure his breaths and tried to relax his muscles, which had all been on high alert to hold him up tall and straight and in command. He was suddenly sleepy, but shot himself a mental order not to be, if for no other reason than he was driving a potential mechanized steel battering ram.

When Robert got to Caltech, he went straight to his office in the Cahill building. He had projects he was working on, he remembered them, he could recall the details, and he got right to it, focusing on the work, trying to think of nothing else, trying not to think the work was utter bullshit. It was a productive morning's work that he was happy with, but he couldn't take seriously. For it was work looking into a quantum mechanics equation that some theorists think indicate that the universe actually had no beginning. The Robert of two weeks ago had felt this to be unlikely, but he had promised a colleague in France that he would play around with the idea. But whether this was real or not, his growing hunger was real and his need to speak to his brother was real, and so he left to meet him for lunch.

8

The brothers met this day at a restaurant located by the Pasadena Del Mar light rail station of the LA Metro A Line. It was across the street from where Richard lived on Raymond Avenue, and he said, muttering at three in the morning, "I ain't walking any farther than that. I have the day off."

"You do?"

"Pulled a long weekend. We had to send several orders to Hercules, positioning it for its next adventure."

The probe was travelling all over the solar system gathering data, precious data.

"Okay, fine, I'll meet you there. Noon?"

"How about noon and a half?"

"Fine."

The restaurant wouldn't have been one that Robert would have chosen. It was not so much the food, which was just a bit less than fine, but rather that it was always crowded and noisy and not the proper place to talk to Richard about what he wanted to talk about. Or reveal. Or confess. So Robert kept the talk small and insignificant as he fought back his headache.

Lunch done, Robert said, "I'll walk you home."

"You'll walk me home? I know I'm you little brother, but really, Bob, I can cross the street by myself."

"I have something I want to talk about. Can we go to your condo?"

"Are you, kidding? It's a mess."

"When isn't it?"

"Hey, it's a bachelor's prerogative."

"Pad." The word had surged through Robert's mind.

"What?"

"Remember? They used to call it a bachelor's pad."

"Did they?"

"I think so."

"Well, I just call it my comfy condo, messy though it might be."

They crossed the street and began the short walk north to the Castle Green, a nationally registered historical monument, a state historical monument, and a designated Pasadena treasure where Richard had his one-bedroom condo. Once the annex to the long-gone Green Hotel, where 19th century well-to-do visitors to Southern California first stayed, having arrived on the Santa Fe Railroad after a long cross-country trip. It had been built in 1898 and now stood seven stories proud as the prime representative of the 19th century in

Pasadena, possibly all of the greater Los Angeles, not known for its historical landmarks.

And certainly, when the brothers walked through the front gate and entered the lush garden-like grounds of the building, it was like crossing a time barrier into that romanticized century. The imposing Moorish Colonial and Spanish style building was fronted by a colonnade veranda through which one accessed the main entrance. An entrance into an even more intense 19th century world, a virtual Victorian atmosphere with many large ground floor reception rooms of various themes including a ballroom, all finely decorated with nothing from the troubled 20th century, and certainly nothing from the so-far rather dull 21st century. It had always amused Robert that his brother, who remotely piloted outer space traveling scientific probes unlocking the secrets of the planets, lived in a fantasy of 19th century genteelness. But then, Richard had always said his favorited authors were from the 19th century whether Jules Verne or Anthony Trollop or Mark Twain or H.G. Wells, or Henry Adams.

"We can sit down here and talk," Richard said. "Why don't we go into the Grand Solon or the Sunroom."

The problem for Robert was that some of other residents were lounging around the Grand Salon, and the other ornately decorated rooms.

"Can we find a little more private space."

Richard looked at his big brother with unmasked concern. "You're not going to tell me you're dying, or anything like that, are you?"

"No!" Robert answered quickly. "I wish it was something that simple."

"Well that's both scary and intriguing."

"You should see it from my eyes."

"Well, we could try the bridge, see if it's empty."

The Bridge was a covered, carpeted and furnished walkway from the front of the building at the second floor to the sidewalk. Originally the bridge extended across Raymond Avenue and was connected with the main Hotel Green building. But now it ended in a bulbus octagon room with two facing couches, some chairs and a radiator. Richard took Robert up to the second floor via the wrought iron man-operated elevator and they entered the bridge from a narrow door. They could see that the octagon room was empty, so they continued to it and both sat on a couch, facing each other.

"Okay, so—hit me with it, brother."

Robert took a breath, a good breath, a breath with plenty of oxygen to fuel what he was going to say. "I'm having a crisis of faith."

"Um—huh?"

"I said, I'm having a crisis of faith."

"You don't have any faith."

"I do now."

"Oh, shit! What, did Aunt Maggie get to you? Did she turn you into a, God-forbid, Christian?"

"No! Of course not! It's not that kind of faith."

"Well, then, faith in what? The Blue Fairy? The goodness of mankind? The Los Angeles Dodgers? No, it can't be that you hate—."

"Richard!"

"Sorry."

"Do you remember last week after lunch when I saw that bright light and then, um, fainted, I guess?"

"You guess?"

"Richard!"

"Of course I remember it, it was only last week. You scared the crap out of me."

"It happened at 1:17 PM on Tuesday April 22 in this year called 2025."

"Ah, okay. I'm glad you remember that so precisely because I forgot to put it down in my diary."

"At that moment, precisely, 1:17 PM on Tuesday April 22 in this year called 2025, that's when the universe came into existence. I know that for a fact. And I have faith that I'm correct."

Richard looked with both concern and confusion at his brother. "Are you saying that—I don't know—that that incident marked a, um, a rebirth for you? That you're a new you, and that's your, you know, new birth date?"

"No, Richard. I'm saying that the universe, all of it, everything that is and, in fact, that we only think ever was, all the matter in the universe, all the helium, all the hydrogen, all the other elements, all of us and any alien others who might be out there, all of it, was created at 1:17 PM on Tuesday April 22 in this year called 2025. That's the revelation, if you want to call it that, that's the information, that's the fact-of-the-matter that I woke up in the hospital knowing."

9

Richard sat forward on the couch and took a moment to think, contemplate, try to digest what his brother had told him, try to make sense of it. But there was no making sense of it. How could there be? Richard reached for his cell phone that was clipped onto his belt, unclipped it, pushed the button to activate the screen, and stared at it.

"What are you doing," Robert said, not understanding why his brother would suddenly need his phone, except maybe to call the good people at the local funny farm.

Very nonchalantly Richard said, "Checking my calendar to make sure we haven't somehow time-warped back to April First. No, no we haven't. But maybe they declared it April Fools Month and I just missed seeing the news on that."

"Ricky," Robert said bringing in their shared history as young brothers, despite now knowing they never were. "I'm not fooling. And I'm no fool. This is my crisis of faith. Not that I've lost faith in the unbelievable, but that I've gained faith in the unbelievable. Unbelievable and stupid and absurd and awful to contemplate. But there it is. I woke up with the, to me, undeniable knowledge that the universe suddenly began at 1:17 PM on Tuesday April 22 in this year called 2025. The spot of bright light was part of it. It becoming an expanding field of burning, bright white that, I don't know, enfolded me, was part of it. It was like, I saw the moment of creation. And that moment was 1:17 PM on Tuesday April 22 in this year called 2025."

"But—but, Robert, seriously, how could that be? We know damn well that that's not true. We have pretty good data that tells us the universe is nearly 14 billion years old. We have a well-established fossil record that tells us how old we humans are, right? Some, what? 200,000 years old."

"Actually, I read a piece last month that said they are now dating *Homo sapiens* back to 300,000 years ago."

"Well, there you go. You're an awfully old fart to be thinking you're only a week old." Richard smiled. It was a weaker smile than he would have liked to flash, for he saw something in his brothers eyes that disturbed.

"And yet—I know for a fact, an indisputable fact, that the universe, maybe all universes came into existence at 1:17 PM on Tuesday April 22 in this year called 2025."

"Stop saying that!" Richard nearly yelled. "Do you want to give me a case of existential angst?"

Robert laughed a slight laugh thinly expelled. "I'm sorry. I know—I know how absurd this sounds. And yet—"

"How? How brother Bob, could this be true? You're being ridiculous!"

"I know that. I know that also for an indisputable fact. But listen—what if—what if the universe was created with its—um—history—uh—attached."

"Attached?"

"Yes. Already there. Which also presupposes, I suppose, that its future is attached. What if the universe was created, or possibly we can say, came into being, as, um, yes, as whole cloth. One thing fully formed, complete, past, present and future already in place, a—a circle, maybe a globe, that we, us, we who can perceive, just travel along a line we call time."

"Are you saying, as some have proposed, that we are not really real, but a computer simulation?"

"Well, I've never bought into that theory before. Why should we be a simulation? What's wrong with just being really real? But being really real should mean—mean—mean what? As opposed to what? I don't know. I just know that at least this universe came into being at 1:17 PM on Tuesday April 22 in this year called 2025. Oh, sorry, you didn't want me to say that anymore."

"That's okay. Maybe it's pre-determined that you're going to say it and there's not a damn thing I can do about it."

"Maybe. Or maybe there truly is randomness in the universe, and I'm one of the random things, suddenly believing what I now believe, although I can hardly believe it."

"You keep talking like that, Bobby, and *I'm* going to get a headache."

Robert did not respond to that but suddenly was quiet and explored something inside his thoughts. Finally he said, "Glitch."

"What?"

"What?"

"You just said glitch."

"I did."

"You did."

"Glitch?"

"That's what you said."

"Yeah! Glitch! It makes sense."

"Well, I'm glad something does."

"I'm a glitch. I wasn't supposed to see the creation of the universe. Like everyone else, I was just supposed to—*uh!*

A stunning pain convinced Robert that his head had just burst. But it hadn't, it remained intact and he, once again loss consciousness.

10

Robert woke up in the hospital again. Elizabeth was sitting close, holding his hand.

"Well, hello, are you back with us?"

"What the—am I in the hospital?"

"Obviously. The second time this month. I'm a bit worried this is becoming a habit," Elizabeth said with a smile that did not completely hide her deep concern.

"The second time?"

"Back in the land of the living, I see." This time it was Richard who brought in two vending machine cups of coffee.

"Richard!" Elizabeth admonished.

"What? I'm sorry."

"Don't tell me I had a near death experience."

"No," Elizabeth quickly said. "You just seem to have lost consciousness again. For no apparent reason, the doctors are still saying. They can't find a damn thing wrong with you. So, nowhere near death, thank goodness."

Robert looked at his wife closely. She had always been a person of self-control, always wonderfully self-possessed. It was something Robert admired about her. She was a woman of strength, emotional strength and intellectual strength. It was a strength he had happily called upon in their early years together during trying times. "And yet you're worried, aren't you, Liz?"

Elizabeth confessed. "Yes. I don't like things happening for no apparent reason. But how are you feeling?"

Robert looked within himself. "Okay, I guess. A little tired, maybe."

"Well, I'm going to go tell the nurse you're awake and see if we can get a doctor in here."

Elizabeth left, taking her cup of coffee with her, and Richard sat down in the chair she had vacated and took a sip of his coffee, then said, "Do you really feel okay now?"

"I guess. I mean, I'm not sure I'm feeling anything. I don't mean I'm numb or anything. I'm just, I don't know, confused, I guess."

"Well, listen. I didn't say anything to Liz."

"About what?"

"What do you mean about what?"

"About whatever you didn't say to Liz."

"Well, about what you were telling me."

"What was I telling you?"

"You know—that crazy shit you were telling me."

"What are you talking about, we were just talking the normal stuff we talk about at lunch."

"No. Not at lunch. After."

"After? Didn't I—you know—faint at lunch? Boy, the restaurant must have been upset."

"What are you talking about? I'm talking about after lunch, when we went to the Castle Green, and talked in the Bridge."

"We went to your building?"

"Sure."

"I don't remember that."

"Well, that's an indication of something going on."

"But what's this crazy shit I was telling you?"

"You don't remember?"

"Damn it, Rick, I wouldn't ask if I did."

"Yeah, I guess not. Well, you know, you were telling me that the universe did not actually begin, you know, thirteen something billion years ago, but, um—you really don't remember this?"

"What?"

"You kept saying that the universe actually began at 1:17 PM on Tuesday April 22 in this year called 2025."

"What? That's crazy!"

"Of course it is, but you kept insisting that it was true, that when you saw that bright light and then collapsed after our lunch last week, that's when the universe actually began, that's when it was actually created. And that was at 1:17 PM on Tuesday April 22 in this year called 2025."

Robert was suddenly dizzy and felt like he was floating on his bed which was twisting and twirling and spinning. And then he regurgitated the bit less than fine food he had had at lunch.

136

11

Elizabeth returned at that moment with a doctor, who yelled down the corridor for a nurse, then rushed to Robert, and found that he was unconscious and dangerously hot. A nurse ran into the room and the doctor ordered her to get Robert cleaned up and in a fresh gown. He asked Elizabeth and Richard to wait outside, then called for another nurse to prepare ice packs.

Once cleaned up, the doctor took Robert's temperature and found it to be 106.9. The nurse with the ice packs ran in and the two nurses proceeded to pack them around Robert's body.

Out in the hallway Elizabeth was white with fear. Richard held her close and suggested they move to the waiting room. She didn't want to, but he insisted.

Back in the room Robert's fever subsided and soon Robert seemed simply to be comfortably asleep and under no distress. Then he opened his eyes, stretched, yawned a long yawn which ended with a satisfied smile as if he had just awakened from a long winter's nap. He looked up and saw the doctor and the two nurses. "Hello," he said. "Are we having a medical convention?"

"How are you feeling Dr. Porter?" The doctor asked.

"Fine," Robert said. "Very fine in fact. I guess I took a long nap, for I feel very rested."

"Hmm," the doctor said then began to prowl over Robert's body with his stethoscope. Then he looked into his eyes. There was nothing amiss. "What's the last thing you remember before you slept?"

"Well, I was having a talk with my brother."

"About what?"

"About the beginning of the universe."

"That's a pretty heady subject, isn't it?"

"Not for me. I'm a cosmologist. The creation and formation of the universe is what I study."

"Oh, I see. And when was the beginning of the universe?"

"It started at 1:17 PM on Tuesday April 22 in this year called 2025, of course." Robert said as if it was something universally known.

"What did you say?" The doctor now had something to be concerned about.

"I said, the best we've pegged it given the data, is that the universe began about 13.8 billion years ago."

"Is that when the Big Bang happened."

"The what?"

"The Big Bang." the doctor said to no comprehension from Robert. "You said the universe began 13.8 billion years ago and I just wondered if that's what they call the Big Bang."

"No, no, that's silly. The universe began at 1:17 PM on Tuesday April 22 in this year called 2025. I ought to know. I was there." Robert grinned. It was a grin of delighted pride, for he was proud that he had been there.

The doctor, a young man, a resident at this hospital, planning to specialize in internal medicine, was desperately thinking what to do. But Robert's grin indicated that maybe...

"Dr. Porter are you, if I may put it crudely, fucking with me?"

"I'm sorry. It may seem that way. Many people can't get there head around how old the universe is, or how we could possibly know it. But you'll just have to trust me as I put my trust in you for medical matters."

"So, tell me again. How old is the universe?"

"Round it out to fourteen billion years. I give community lectures on this all the time. You should come to one."

"Yes, I would love to."

"I'm cold."

"We put ice packs around you. You had a dangerously high fever there for a moment."

"I did?"

"Yes."

"I don't remember.'

"Well, it came on suddenly, but we got in under control. But it does indicate that we need to do some more tests. I'm going to talk to your primary doctor and come up with a plan. In the meantime, I think we'll keep you over night."

"Well, okay. I hope dinner includes butterscotch pudding. I used to love butterscotch pudding when I was a kid."

12

When the doctor, whose name was Doody, talked to Robert's primary care physician, whose name was Ess, he asked him if Robert had had any history of mental illness. Dr. Ess answered that no; there was nothing in his record. Robert Porter was a highly educated man of exceptional intelligence.

"Doesn't mean he's not nuts," Dr. Doody said with a lack of good medical etiquette. "Let me explain what he's been saying."

13

Exponentially many millions of millennia adding up to tremendous trillions of years and certainly so long after the death of our sun and obviously our Earth but not quite fully 1,000,000,000,000,000,000,000,000,000,000,000, 000,000,000,000,000,000,000,000,000,000,000,0 00,000 years from now, the Replicator had finished his work sitting on one of the last vestiges of coherent matter being held together by a force unfathomable to any entity existing in the long past of which there was so much more than the very short future ahead.

At least he would be finished if he could just get that last infinitesimally tiny imperfection in his work that he almost failed to see, but, yep, there it was that——that, stupid little glitch! But try hard as he might, he just couldn't make his replication any better than it was.

"Does it matter?" the Chronicler, who had fed the Replicator all the information he had needed to make his replica, asked.

"Does it matter? All matter matters, what's the matter with you? Of course it matters!"

"But does it matter enough?"

"Well..."

"Yes?"

"I wanted it to be perfect."

"If the universe had been perfect—at least from our selfish point-of-view—we wouldn't be clinging on to this last bit of matter surrounded by deeply dark and cold disintegration."

"True."

"So?"

"So—okay—I guess it will do."

"Okay."

"But, still, I almost had it. I thought I fixed the glitch for a moment. But then, there it was again. It's been quite frustrating."

"Look, we don't have much time. Literally! It's getting colder! It's getting darker! It's getting more and more nothing each dying second that we debate. The point of this project was not to recreate our universe perfectly, but to make a memory of it coherent enough to send off to other universes so that we might not be forgotten."

"Yeah, well, I've always seen a flaw in that thinking."

"A flaw? What flaw?"

"None of the other universes know of our existence, and if you are not known, it only follows that you can't be forgotten."

The Chronicler had to think about that for a precious moment. Finally, he said, "That's the saddest thing I've ever heard in my life."

"Yeah, I know."

"Well, then the goal is to introduce ourselves, then, to leave behind some evidence that we existed. A handprint, so to speak, to make our mark on the multiverse."

"Okay. I can get behind that."

"Even if it's not perfect?"

"Well, it is such a little glitch, I suppose..."

"Then duplicate your replication and send it out now over and over and over in the hope that other universes will pick it up and know that we had been here."

"Okay. I just wish—"

"Do it!"

"Geez, you don't have to bite my head off!"

"What do you care? You've got two others."

END

(of the universe?)

ABOUT THE AUTHOR
STEVEN PAUL LEIVA

Before publishing fourteen critically acclaimed works of fiction, award-winning and Amazon Bestselling author Steven Paul Leiva spent over twenty years in the entertainment industry as a writer and producer. He worked with such talent as Academy Award-winning producer Richard Zanuck; director Ivan

Reitman; literary legend and screenwriter Ray Bradbury; Star Wars producer Gary Kurtz; Looney Tunes legend Chuck Jones; and Animation Feature Academy Award-winning director Brad Bird. He even lent his voice to the Academy Award shortlisted (placing in the top ten) animated short, "The Indescribable Nth."

Leiva produced the animation for the original *Space Jam,* starring the very tall Michael Jordan and the relatively short Bugs Bunny. For this production, Leiva assembled an ad hoc animation studio for Warner Bros and executive producer Ivan Reitman in three days over the phone.

During this time, he wrote novels and a play, *Made on the Moon,* which premiered at the Edinburgh Festival Fringe, receiving a four-star review from *The Scotsman.*

After *Space Jam*, Leiva decided to concentrate on writing novels. Since 2003, he has published thirteen novels, a novella, and a book of essays.

His work has been praised by literary great Ray Bradbury, Oscar-winning film producer Richard Zanuck, New York Times bestselling author and Pulitzer Prize finalist Diane Ackerman, New York Times Bestselling Author Jonathan Maberry, comedy great Phil Proctor of The Firesign Theater, USA Today Bestselling Author Jean Rabe, *Star Trek: Enterprise* actor John Billingsley, Australian philosopher Russell Blackford, and British physicist and author Stephen Webb. He has received the Scribe Award from the International Association of Media Tie-in Writers.

BOOKS BY STEVEN PAUL LEIVA

Blood is Pretty: The First Fixxer Adventure

Meet the Fixxer—with wit and aplomb he works the fruitful fields of Hollywood fixing the sins and correcting the stupidities of the denizens therein. In *Blood is Pretty* he comes to the rescue of "the most beautiful woman I have ever seen" to extricate her from the grip of the soul-sucking sexual desires of a producer born in slime, and takes on the task of buying off with money and muscle a film geek who won't cooperate with a director of minuscule talent who simply wants to claim "V"—the geek's "Holy Grail" of a film treatment—as his own.

Hollywood is an All-Volunteer Army: The Second Fixxer Adventure

What those in the know in Hollywood really know is that if they need a dark deed done, if they need a sticky personal or professional problem "fixed," they can call upon the mysterious and dangerous Fixxer. Whether you are a successful comedy film director whose "Art" has never truly been appreciated because the country's most important film critic has held a grudge against you since college, or you are a neophyte and naïve screenwriter who resents the professional blackmail she has just suffered, you call upon the Fixxer.

Traveling in Space

A unique first contact novel from the aliens' point-of-view. The last thing the factfinders— who call themselves Life—expected to find while traveling in space in "The Curious" on a mission from their planet, The Living World, was other life. But one day, they stumble upon the third planet out from a backwater sun and find it teeming with a vast diversity of life, including one sentient and cognizant, if primitive, species that they dub Otherlife. Being not only from The Curious but inherently curious themselves, they begin to study the Otherlife and their alien culture, discovering such strange things as marriage, intoxicating drinks, weapons of minor and mass destruction, the gleeful inhaling of toxic substances, two-parent families, layered language, genocide, non-nude bathing, and—the strangest thing of all— religion.

This first contact between Life and Otherlife, disconcerting for both, has moments of humor and moments of horror—and neither escape the encounter unchanged.

12 Dogs of Christmas - A Novelization

Winner of the Scribe Award from the International Association of Media Tie-in Authors

Based on the beloved independent family film.

12-year-old Emma O'Connor is sent to live with her "aunt" in the small town of Doverville. Emma soon finds herself in the middle of a "dogfight" with the mayor and town dogcatcher. In order to strike down their "no-dogs" law, Emma must bring together a group of schoolmates, grown-ups, and adorable dogs of all shapes and sizes in a spectacular holiday pageant. *The 12 Dogs of Christmas* is a fun, heartwarming story featuring a diverse canine cast and is perfect for all those who love dogs, kids, and Christmas.

By the Sea: A Comic Novel

A modern comic adult fairy tale with an ensemble cast of Cinderellas. Instead of a kingdom by the sea, our story takes place in and around a residential hotel by the sea. The architecturally eclectic Briers Hotel is situated on Leech Beach, a not particularly inviting beach that is often fog-bound and always scruffy. But it's the perfect setting for our Cinderellas, male, and female, who put up with the scruffiness of life while striving to make it through their various personal seaside fogs. Theater; art; antiques; old movies; sex; more sex; death; fast and slow cars, chicken shit, and cow poop; military bearing and erotic emissions—not to mention the wicked witch, the sea serpent by the seashore, the village ogre, the village idiot, and several Prince Charmings—all figure into this merry tale with a multitude of happy endings.

IMP: A Political Fantasia
(Revised Edition)

Thomas P. Powell's ascension in politics was both unusual and very American. From traffic cop to Vice President of the United States, his climb up the ladder of public service was often due to the push of random acts and not-so-happy accidents—although Thomas held the opinion that it was due solely to his singular innate moral

authority. What matters is what's within, that's

the Powell political philosophy. Then, on the cusp of his grasping the last rung of the American political ladder, something truly within suddenly appears. A horrible homunculus, an impetuous imp, climbs out of Thomas's right ear to bedevil his nights, confuse his days, and take him on a crazy, wild, nauseating, and nuclear journey. It's as if *The West Wing* was done as a *Twilight Zone* episode.

Journey to Where: A Contemporary Scientific Romance

When a radical experiment into the nature of time is sabotaged, the scientific team finds themselves in an alternate universe and where humans never became the dominant life force. Instead, dinosaurs evolved into intelligent bipeds, developing language and societal structures.

The scientists must learn to communicate with this alien species, who view them as unusual pets, and figure out how to recreate the original experiment in a non-industrialized world so they can go back home—assuming there's a home, or even a universe, to return to. But the scientist who sabotaged them is trapped in this new worldwith them. And he's looking to rise to power, even if his quest means the death of his traveling companions. A contemporary scientific romance in the tradition of H. G. Wells and Jules Verne

Creature Feature: A Horrid Comedy

THERE IS SOMETHING STRANGE HAPPENING IN PLACIDVILLE!

It is 1962. Kathy Anderson, a serious actress

who took her training at the Actors Studio in New York is stuck playing Vivacia, the Vampire Woman on Vivacia's House of Horrors for a local Chicago TV station. Finally fed up showing old monster movies to creature feature fans, she quits and heads to New York, and the fame and footlights of Broadway.

She stops off to visit her parents and old friends in Placidville, the all-American, middle-class, blissfully normal Midwest small town she grew up in. But she finds things are strange in Placidville. Kathy's parents, her best friend from high school, the local druggist, and even the Oberhausen twins are all acting curiously creepy, odiously odd, and wholly weird. Especially the town's super geeky nerd, Gerald, who warns of dark days ahead.

Has Kathy entered a zone in the twilight? Did she reach the limits that are outer? Has she fallen through a mirror that is black? Or is it just—just—politics as usual?

Bully 4 Love: A Rather Odd Love Story

Adolphus Seruya is a happy, middle-aged, unambitious bachelor and a history professor at a prominent community college. Then suddenly SHE walks into his classroom. Lavinia Carson is beautiful in a unique yet compelling way. And radiant almost beyond description. Thus begins a rather odd story of love rejected, love ignored, love found—and cuttlefish pizza.

Extraordinary Voyages

Award-winning, Amazon Bestselling author Steven Paul Leiva is your tour guide to some of the strange destinations he has traveled over the years.

In *Made on the Moon*, travel with Leiva into the mind of one Stanley Lewis, a little man with a big dream. He had wanted to go to the Moon from the time he was an infant. Not a toddler, not a child, not a young man, but a babe in his mother's arms.

Then go even deeper into Stanley's mind as Leiva takes you to the poetic realm of this little man's mind by presenting "What a Pleasure it's Been to Piss in Porcelain: The Rude Poems of Stanley Lewis. "As you might guess, you don't want to read these poems to your mother.

Next stop—Mars! We are joined on the tour by Cyrano De Bergerac and Baron Munchausen in the year 1641. Although the Baron is actually from 1790. A weird situation for historical personages. But then Cyrano and the Baron were also fictional characters. An imaginative tale about real imaginative gentlemen on a surreal trip tripping over the real.

Then two short stops to conclude our voyages. You won't even need an overnight bag.

The Reluctant Heterosexual
A Tragicomedy In Four Movements A Prelude And An Interlude

With *The Reluctant Heterosexual,* Steven Paul Leiva concludes his thematic trilogy: **The Love, Sex and Pursuit of Happiness Novels**. All three novels look at these essential aspects of the human condition, with each novel focusing on one of the three. *By the Sea: A Comic Novel* looks at our unease when unhappy. *Bully 4 Love: A*

Rather Odd Love Story takes a skewed view of this most revered emotion. And now, *The Reluctant Heterosexual,* as the title predicts, concerns sex, which is not always the same as love, nor is it always a happy situation.

Subtitled *A Tragicomedy in Four Movements a Prelude and an Interlude,* each section of the novel, as in a musical composition, has its own tempo, mood, and form as it tells the story— and stories—of Robert Leslie Cromwell and Sandy Smith. Two *Homo sapiens* surviving and striving in the late 20th century.

Robert and Sandy are intelligent, creative, not unattractive, wealthy, married to each other, and in love. And yet their procreating bodies might as well be standing naked on a savanna in Africa in the late Pliocene Era.

It's the sometimes-comical conflict between

ancient bodies and modern culture. Can there possibly be a happy ending?

Right: Portrait of a Controversy

In a 1980s America different from our own, both familiar and not, Congress passed and President Henshaw signed the Birth Cessation Act. Once it became law, no one would be allowed to have a child for twenty-five years, any woman under 24 weeks pregnant was required to have an immediate abortion, and all men were called up to report for a vasectomy.

"Conscious regulation of human numbers must be achieved." Dr. Paul R. Ehrlich wrote in his 1968 bestseller, *The Population Bomb*. By the early 80s, the government had statistical projections that the population growth was outpacing the available resources needed for all in America to live a comfortable and secure life. A situation that would inevitably lead to the chaos and violence of extreme civil unrest.

Most Americans, liking comfort and security, supported the government's action. Most, but not all. And those who didn't, including a world-famous female billionaire entrepreneur/inventor/film producer, a major appliance salesman from Queens, a well-to-do Manhattan college radical, an unwed mother in Los Angeles who protests most horribly, America's premier pundit-columnist, and a young man who talks to his dead brother, became loud enough to start a fresh new controversy in America.

This is a portrait of that controversy.

The Person Who Hated People

Retired History professor C.D. Beekman is known by the townspeople of Madison, California, as "the nicest man." He's always friendly and has kind words for everyone. When Professor Beekman prevents a mass murder at the local mall, he becomes famous far beyond Madison—he becomes a national celebrity. And when he puts forth the simple philosophy that *Mass Murder isn't Nice*, he is dubbed "Mr. Nice Guy." But is he? Is he truly Mr. Nice Guy? Or is he The Person Who Hated People? You decide.

Joyce Takes Over The World
A Surreally Realistic Fantasy Novella

"If I ruled the world..." was the refrain often heard coming from the lips of Joyce Bullock, four years beyond the age of fifty, only three pounds over the weight she should have been, five-foot-seven with brown hair not yet gone grey. She was happily divorced. Or, rather, she refused to be unhappy just because her husband had left her for a younger woman. She felt herself well rid of him, not because of the infidelity, but because his action was such a cliché. Joyce hated clichés. As she hated many things in the world, which seemed to be conspiring every day to piss her off. And so, "If I ruled the world..." was her mantra.

Then, one fine Spring day, the Universe decides to take a vacation and hands over the keys—metaphorically speaking—to Joyce. And so, what choice did she have? Joyce took over the world.

Searching for Ray Bradbury: Writings about the Writer and the Man

Includes the title piece written for the *Los Angeles Times*, and "The Man Who Was Himself," Leiva's memorial appreciation of Bradbury commissioned by the Science Fiction & Fantasy Writers of America for the Winter 2012/13 edition of their quarterly magazine, *The Bulletin*. Other pieces were originally written for *Neworld Review*, KCET.org, and his personal blog.

With a special foreword by Hugo and Nebula Award-winning author David Brin.

THANK YOU FOR READING

TO BEGIN AT THE BEGINNING

A Novella

With a Beginning, a Middle, and an End